The Dinosaur Who Slammed the Door

Russell Punter

Illustrated by Andy Elkerton

In this story, you'll meet Max. He's always feeling stressed.

Here's his dad,

school helper, Sid

32 × 2 =

and Max's
classmate, Tess.

Max slams the front door – CRASH!

Dad pulls up
outside the school.

Max slams the car door – CRUNCH!

Lessons will be starting soon.

Max will have to dash.

He shuts his locker –
SMASH!

Max races to his classroom.

Sid's taking charge today.

"I'll test you on your sums," he says.

Max groans and moans, "No way!"

"What's nine plus three plus eight?" asks Sid.

Er, twenty-one?

Fourteen?

"Oh, I *hate* doing sums!" Max shouts.

Calm down. Don't make a scene!

Next, there comes
a music class.

Max tries to blow the trumpet, but...

...he just can't make a sound.

Max stomps across
the floor.

"Now, Max…" starts Sid.
The lunch bell rings.

Max leaves and
SLAMS the door.

Inside the cafeteria,

Max settles down for lunch.

He grabs a sandwich
from his box...

...and quickly
starts to munch.

"Yuck – sardine and shrimp!" says Max.

He SLAMS his lunchbox
on the floor...

and storms out in a huff.

Max gets stressed
all afternoon.

SPLAT!

BANG!

WALLOP!

SLAM!

"Max needs to change his ways," thinks Sid

and comes up with a plan.

The next day, when
Max gets to school...

...he sees a face that's new.

Max thinks Tess is super cool.

So Tess pulls off her hat.

"How come you weren't annoyed?" Max asks.

Tess smiles.
"Why bother, Max?"

"Little things don't make me mad."

"Tess, what's nine times five?" asks Sid.

Er, forty-eight... no, nine!

"The answer's forty-five,"
says Sid.

Tess doesn't lose
her cool all day.

She doesn't scream
or shout.

It makes Max stop
and start to think.

Perhaps I *should* chill out?

The next day, Max sets off for school.

DINO 10

He opens the front door...

...then shuts it gently, with a click.

He's not stressed anymore.

"Thanks, Dad! It will be great." Max shuts the car door with a swish...

...and strolls in through the gate.

When Sid asks Max
to answer sums...

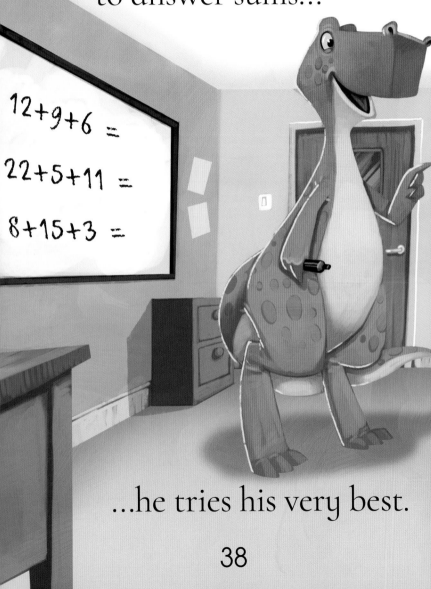

...he tries his very best.

And even though he
gets one wrong –

he doesn't get upset.

The music lesson
comes around.

Max finds it hard
once more.

But now he doesn't
throw a fit

or stomp across
the floor.

41

All day long, Max
keeps his cool.

His classmates like
him more now, too.

He leaves school
with a smile.

Max passes Sid,
outside his house.

He stops to say hello. "Tess
didn't come to school today.

Where was she?
Do you know?"

"Come on inside," adds Sid.

Series editor: Lesley Sims

Reading consultant: Alison Kelly

First published in 2023 by Usborne Publishing Limited, 83-85 Saffron Hill, London EC1N 8RT, United Kingdom. usborne.com Copyright © 2023 Usborne Publishing Limited. The name Usborne and the Balloon logo are registered trade marks of Usborne Publishing Limited.

Look out for all the great stories in the Dinosaur Tales series!

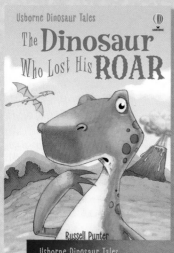

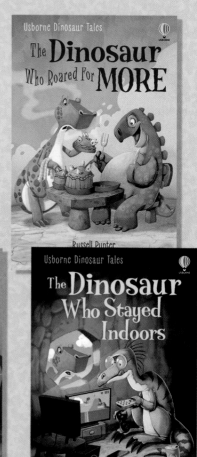

They're totally roar-some!